Suppertime for E

by Harriet Ziefert • illustrated by Nor

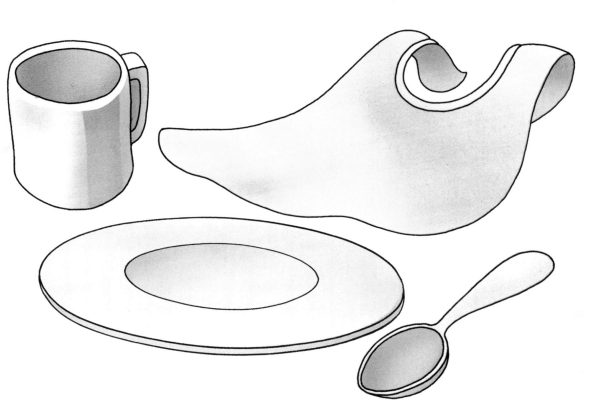

Random House 🏠 New York

Illustrations copyright © 1985 by Norman Gorbaty. Text copyright © 1985 by Harriet Ziefert. All rights reserved under International and Pan-American Copyright Conventions. Published in the United States by Random House, Inc., New York, and simultaneously in Canada by Random House of Canada Limited, Toronto. Library of Congress Catalog Card Number: 84-61324   ISBN: 0-394-87024-7   Manufactured in the Netherlands   1 2 3 4 5 6 7 8 9 0

BABY BEN is a trademark of North American Thought Combine, Inc.

Ready for supper, Baby Ben?
Here's your bib.
And here's your plate, your spoon,
and your cup.

Now you're all ready!

Baby Ben, taste these carrots . . .

just like a hungry bunny rabbit!

Does the bunny like the carrot?
Open this page and take a peek!

"Sniff! Sniff!
My carrot is all gone!

Please, may I have
some of yours?"

Have some hamburger . . .

just like a hungry puppy dog!

"Bow-wow!
My meat is all gone!

Please, may I have
some of yours?"

Drink some milk . . .

just like a hungry kitty cat!

"**Meow! Meow!**
My milk is all gone!

Please, may I have
some of yours?"

Take a bite of banana . . .

just like a hungry little monkey!

"Screep!
Screep!
My banana
is all gone!

Please, may I have
some of yours?"

Okay, Baby Ben.
Now you can have your ice cream . . .

just like a hungry little pig!

"Oink! Oink!
My ice cream is all gone.

Please, may I have
some of yours?"

"All

Gone!”

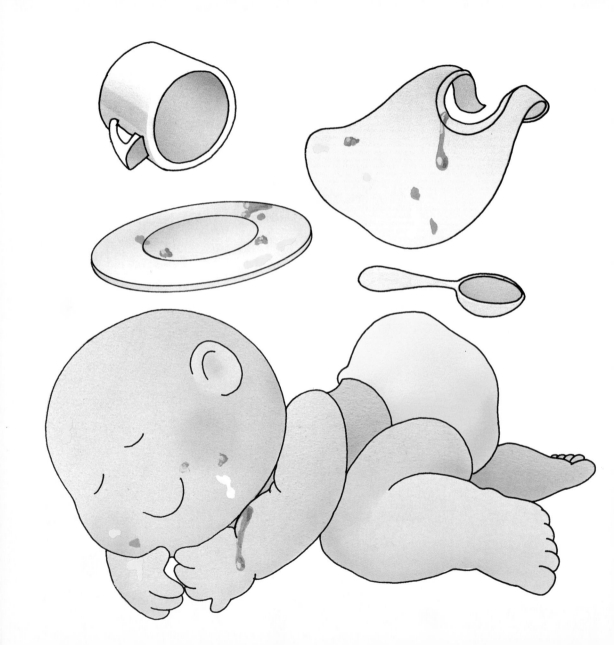